Ein Stein: The Chipmunk Who Became an Astronaut

BY UNCLE ANDY

Eloquent Books

Eloquent Books
An imprint of Strategic Book Group
P.O.Box 333
Durham, CT 06422

www.StrategicBookGroup.com

ISBN: 978-1-60911-209-7

All photos couresty of Wikipedia except as follows:
Leif Knutsen—GNU Free Documentation License: page 2
Jan van der Crabben—Creative Commons: pages 3, 25
NASA: pages 13, 19
Wikipedia Commons—Pearson Scott Foresman: page 14
Creative Commons ShareAlike 2.0 License: page 24
David Iliff —Creative Commons Attribution ShareAlike 3.0
License: page 25

Printed in the United States of America

This book is dedicated to my wife, Bernice, who has endured her husband for fifty-nine years, and to my daughters, Sharon and Terri.

When I was at home, I was in a better place.

—Shakespeare, *As You Like It*, II, iv

Contents

Chapter 1
Life at Home

He lived in a dark, dingy, damp, and dismal hole. He was miserable, bored, and restless. He longed to leave home and see the rest of the world.

His name was Ein, an unusual name. It was a nickname given to him by his parents, Mr. and Mrs. Stein, because he was always asking questions such as, "Why do small stones sink and large boats float?" and "How do flies walk upside down on the ceiling?" They laughed at this, and decided to call him Ein Stein because he was always curious about the world around him, just like the famous scientist, Albert Einstein.

Ein

He lived with his two brothers and two sisters; Edwin, Ethan, Elizabeth, and Eleanor along with his father, Olley, and his mother, Olga. They lived in the roots of a two hundred-year-old oak tree.

One of his chores was to dig new tunnels beneath the tree. He had to carry the diggings far away from the tree. His father had ordered him not to dump them just outside at their camouflaged entrance or this would alert their enemies as to their whereabouts. Another of his chores was to carry water for the family from the river nearby.

Ein's Home

It was not easy, because he found water to be very heavy. All this work was another reason he longed to leave home and go elsewhere.

He had to admit, though, that he did enjoy playing in the hay with his brothers and sisters.

Ein's Hay Field

His father hid all sorts of goodies; nuts, berries, seeds, and mushrooms in the hay and they would race to see who could find the most.

Even though he had good times like these, Ein was still anxious to leave home and see the rest of the world.

Chapter 2

He Begins His Journey

One day, after his ablutions, Ein felt bold, confident, and adventurous so he decided to leave home. Because of his small stature and a crook in his neck, he could not see much above his head but he didn't think that would hamper his travels. After a long walk, he saw what he thought was a funny wall.

It has holes in it! he thought.

(It was a chain link fence.)

How is that supposed to keep things out? he wondered as he proceeded to crawl through one of the holes.

When he got to the other side he saw two legs walking and he decided to follow them.

He followed the legs which disappeared behind what looked like two doors.

As he got in one door, another door moved behind him and he was forced to move around in a circle. He decided he had to get out at the next opportunity. When he did, he found he was right back outside where he started from!

What happened? he wondered.

Do you know what happened?

He decided to try again. This time he got out earlier and found himself inside a large room. Ahead of him, he saw two doors sliding open with a room on the other side. He saw the legs walk into that room and he followed them.

When he got in, the doors closed and he heard a whirring noise. He felt his stomach sink and his knees bend.

He didn't know where he was.

Do you where he was?

Do you know why his stomach sank and his knees bent?

Answers: He had entered a revolving door.; He was in an elevator.; The elevator was going up and increasing his gravity. Normally you might weigh 100 pounds [or 45 kilograms], but when the elevator rises you weigh about 115 pounds [or 52 kilograms].

Chapter 3

He Goes Too Far

When he got off the elevator he saw some more legs with orange pants and black boots.

Why do they have orange pants and where are they going? he wondered.

He decided to follow them and entered another room. Then he heard the door close behind him.

He heard someone counting backwards, "five, four, three, two, one," and then a huge roar so loud that he had to plug his ears and the whole room shook terribly.

He felt his stomach sink and his knees bend just like in the elevator only more so. Then, when he opened his eyes, he realized he had been asleep or had lost consciousness. He wondered what had happened.

Do you know what had happened?

Do you know why the astronauts don't pass out during lift-off?

Answer: He had wandered into a space shuttle which had taken off with a roar. On liftoff his weight had increased tremendously due to the increase in gravity. If he had weighed 100 pounds [or 45 kilograms] normally, the liftoff would have increased his weight to about 300 pounds [or 136 kilograms]. This caused all the blood in his head to fall into his legs, so he passed out. Astronauts don't pass out during liftoff because they lie down with their legs above their heads.

Chapter 4
A Weird Place!

He found himself on the ceiling of a room! He was no longer on the floor!

How come I'm up here? he wondered.

Do you know why he was on the ceiling?

Now he could look down and see everything.

"Now how do I get down there?" he said to himself.

On the ground, I pressed down to jump up, so maybe if I press up, I'll go down? he thought.

So he pushed against the ceiling and floated down to the floor.

"That was fun!" he said. "Let's see how high I can jump."

At home he could barely jump over one of the large

roots of the oak tree. He leapt into the air and crashed into the ceiling! "Wow!" he said. "I wonder if I can do a somersault?"

He leapt up while pushing backwards and did a complete somersault.

"Cool!" he cried. "Wait till I tell Ethan about this!"

Then he noticed a round window on the wall and went over to look out.

Image courtesy of Wikipedia

This is what he saw:

"Wow! I'm really far from home now!"

What was it?

Answers: In space, there is no gravity to hold him on to the floor, so he could float around in the room.; The planet Earth with its white clouds and blue ocean.

Chapter 5

He Makes Friends

He decided to look around some more and came upon this:

Image courtesy of NASA

As he was wondering what it was, he heard a voice behind him, "Well little fellow, where did you come from? And what's your name?"

Ein was a little surprised and apprehensive at meeting someone, but he answered, "Ein Stein, sir, I got lost."

"Ah! The same name as the famous scientist eh? My name is Chris Hadfield, one of the astronauts on board. If you're wondering what you're looking at, it's the controls to steer the space shuttle."

"Oh, just like an airplane?"

"No, a plane uses ailerons to steer with."

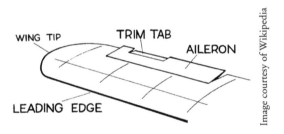

"The ailerons turn against the airflow and bank or turn the plane. But in space there is no air, so they use jets to steer the shuttle. Here, I'll show you."

Chris took out a balloon and blew it up.

"Now hold onto the tip of the balloon, then point it to the left and let some air out."

Ein did as Chris directed. Because he weighed so little, the discharge of the balloon sent him to the right side of the shuttle!

"Wow! That's the cat's pajamas!" said Ein, remembering what his father often said when he really liked something!

Then he pointed the tip to the right and went back to the left!

"Now I see how it works!" said Ein. "Watch this!" He counted down "five, four, three, two, one," then pointed it behind him and opened the neck of the balloon wide open. "Liftoff!" he cried. The balloon made a loud squirting "*fffffittttt*" sound and he sped away quite fast.

He was heading for a crash into the control desk, but instead, he went head first into someone's stomach, another astronaut, a lady astronaut!

"Ein, let me introduce you to Julie Payette," said Chris.

"Hello there," said Julie. "You're cute."

You're pretty cute yourself! thought Ein.

"How did you get on board?" asked Julie.

"He got lost," said Chris.

"You look like you're thirsty after all that jetting about. Would you like a drink?" offered Julie.

Julie Payette

"Okay, thanks," agreed Ein.

Aside to Chris, Julie whispered, "Shall we play the drink trick?"

"Yes, let's," whispered Chris.

Julie brought a glass of water with a lid on top, took the lid off, then very carefully holding the glass, she offered Ein a drink of water.

When Ein took the glass and raised it up to his mouth to drink he got a real surprise!

The water floated up and away into the room!

"What happened to the water?" he said.

"That's a trick we play on new astronauts," laughed Julie. "Because there is no gravity here, the water doesn't fall into your mouth so we have to drink our water from a bag with a straw."

Ein, always curious, asked, "Where do you get your water? You haven't got a river. And water is very heavy to carry. It would take an awful lot of energy to carry a lot of water. If you were away for a long time you would run out of water and you might all die of thirst!"

"Well," explained Julie, "we use the same water over and over again. All the water we use, and I mean all the water, is filtered and chemically treated so that it can be used again for drinking, eating, and washing."

"Even the pee?" asked Ein.

"Yes, even that," said Chris.

"Now, how about that drink of water from a straw?" asked Julie with a smirk.

"No thanks," said Ein, making a face, "I've changed my mind."

"Actually," said Chris, "the water is better than you get from a tap at home!"

"Okay," said Ein, "if you say so."

He drank some and agreed it was okay.

"What about poo? Do you reuse it too?"

"Oh no," said Chris, "we store it in a tank and open the tank to space to dry and freeze it. Later, we let it out into the atmosphere where it burns up. So next time you see a beautiful shooting star, that's what it might be!"

Chapter 6

Learning How to Eat and Sleep

Ein ate dinner with the astronauts that evening.

"Could I have a piece of toast, please," asked Ein.

Image courtesy of NASA

Astronaut Tony Antonelli Eating Dinner

"Sure," said Chris. "Let me get it ready for you."

Then Chris brought it in a bag and showed Ein how to suck it out of the bag.

It was the soggiest piece of toast Ein had ever tasted!

"Yuk!" he cried, and spit it out where it immediately floated up to the ceiling.

"Ein," Chris admonished, "we've got to be very careful here and not allow things to float into the air. Otherwise, we could have many nasty, unhealthy things in the air we breathe. That's why we can't have toast as we know it or the crumbs could float away. We have to mix all our food with water in a bag so we can suck it out."

"Here," Julie offered, "try this chocolate pudding. You'll like it better."

Ein did enjoy it more and was deeply grateful to Julie.

Then Julie said, "It's time for bed. Chris and I will show you where we sleep."

"Would you please tuck me in," pleaded Ein.

"Okay," said Chris.

"Not you, Chris."

"Okay," said Julie. "I'll do it."

She proceeded to show Ein how to strap himself to the bed so that he wouldn't float away during the night. Then she gave Ein a hug, a goodnight kiss, and both astronauts left the room.

Wow! She kissed me, thought Ein, as he drifted into a deep sleep. He had fallen in love. During the night he dreamed he was back at home at his haystack and he and Julie were throwing soggy pieces of toast at Chris.

Chapter 7

A Scary Return

Next day, after breakfast, he knew he had to poo and wondered how. He knew he couldn't do it inside. So he floated around till he found what looked like a toilet.

I wonder how you go here? he thought.

"Well, when you have to go, you have to go," he said to himself.

So he floated up to sit on the edge of the toilet seat. *I wonder how you flush here?* he wondered as he looked around for the handle to flush water into the toilet.

There were all kinds of buttons to push but no handle. He reached over and pushed one of the large buttons.

Suddenly, a loud, ominous, sucking sound, emanated from the toilet!

Ein couldn't withstand the pull of the suction, teetered on the edge, and then tumbled down into the toilet bowl! Not only that, but a hole in the bottom of the bowl opened and he tumbled straight down through it. And then it closed!

"Oh no!" he cried, as he imagined where he was.

Is this the end?

Am I going to rot away here?

In the dark?

On top of a pile of poo?

But wait!

It's not soft, gooey, and sticky. It doesn't smell! It's dry and you can walk on it!

Then he remembered that Chris had said the poo was stored, then opened to space, where it was freeze-dried. Then he looked up and saw a light in the distance. He ran up the pile of dried poo and looked out through the opening to the sky.

This is what he saw:

"I don't want to go there!" he cried.

Then he waited to see what would come next and this was his next view:

Image courtesy of David Iliff

"I know where that is!" he shouted.

(Luckily for Ein the space shuttle was about to land. Otherwise, he would be dried up and frozen by now!)

He leapt out the opening and the speed of the space shuttle carried him forward and gravity carried him downward. He used his legs and paws as ailerons to

Image courtesy of Jan van der Crabben

steer with and landed— guess where?

On his own little haystack!

He ran home and all his family came out to

meet him.

He was so very glad and relieved to be back home again with his family.

"Where were you?" they asked.

When he told them that he had been farther away than most people have gone, and about his somersault, and about jet steering with a balloon, and about his girl friend. Most of them were skeptical.

Especially Edwin who said, "Yeah, and yesterday I rode an elephant!"

But his father seemed to believe him. He was very glad to have his son home, gave him a big hug, and noted that Ein was very lucky to have survived.

"Look, son," he said, "in the future, you'll have to be more cautious and less bold. You know, there is a saying that you should remember—Some people are old and some are bold. But there are no old bold people!"

Biographies

Julie Payette

Julie was born on October 20, 1963 in Montreal, Quebec, Canada. She enjoys running, skiing, racquet sports, and scuba diving. She has a Commercial Pilot License, can speak six languages, plays the piano, and has sung with various symphonic orchestras. She is married and has two children—(sorry Ein).

She has a Bachelor of Engineering degree in Electrical Engineering and a Master of Applied Science degree in Computer Engineering.

Image courtesy of Wikipedia

Chris Hadfield (top right) with Fellow Astronauts

The crew assigned to the STS-74 mission included (seated left to right) James D. Halsell, pilot and Kenneth D. Cameron, commander. Standing, left to right, are mission specialists William S. McArthur, Jerry L. Ross, and Chris A. Hadfield.

Chris was born on August 29, 1959 in Sarnia, Ontario, Canada. He is married with three children. He enjoys skiing, playing the guitar, singing, riding, writing, running, playing volleyball and squash, (and making soggy toast).

He has a Bachelor of Science Degree in Mechanical Engineering and a Master of Science in Aviation. He was a recipient of the Top Pilot graduate of the USAF Test Pilot School and U.S. Navy Test Pilot of the Year, 1991.